Alligator Alley

A WOODLAND MYSTERY
By Irene Schultz

Wright Group
McGraw-Hill

To my sister-in-law Ellen Goldstein, strong, kind, bright, and daring

Alligator Alley
Copyright ©2000 Wright Group/McGraw-Hill
Text by Irene Schultz
Cover illustrations by Meg Aubrey
Cameo illustrations by Taylor Bruce
Interior illustrations by Tom Sperling and Adam Weiskind

Woodland Mysteries® is a registered trademark of
Wright Group/McGraw-Hill.

Wright Group/McGraw-Hill
19201 120th Avenue NE, Suite 100
Bothell, WA 98011
www.WrightGroup.com

Printed in the United States of America

10 9 8 7 6 5 4 3

ISBN: 0-322-01959-1
ISBN: 0-322-02372-6 (6-pack)

What family solves mysteries ... has adventures all over the world ... and loves oatmeal cookies?

It's the Woodlanders!

Sammy Westburg (10 years old)
His sister Kathy Westburg (13)
His brother Bill Westburg (14)
His best friend Dave Briggs (16)
His best grown-up friend Mrs. Tandy
And Mop, their little dog!

The children all lost their parents, but with Mrs. Tandy have made their own family.

Why are they called the Woodlanders? Because they live in a big house in the Bluff Lake woods. On Woodland Street!

Together they find fun, mystery, and adventure. What are they up to now?

Read on!

Meet the Woodlanders!

Sammy Westburg
Sammy is a ten-year-old wonder! He's big for his fifth-grade class, and big-mouthed, too. He has wild hair and makes awful spider faces. Even so, you can't help liking him.

Bill Westburg
Bill, fourteen, is friendly and strong, and only one inch taller than his brother Sammy. He loves Sammy, but pokes him to make him be quiet! He's in junior high.

Kathy Westburg
Kathy, thirteen, is small, shy, and smart. She wants to be a doctor some day! She loves to be with Dave, and her brothers kid her about it. She's in junior high, too.

Dave Briggs

Dave, sixteen, is tall and blond. He can't walk, so he uses a wheelchair and drives a special car. He likes coaching high-school sports, solving mysteries, and reading. And Kathy!

Mrs. Tandy

Sometimes the kids call her Mrs. T. She's Becky Tandy, their tall, thin, caring friend. She's always ready for a new adventure, and for making cookies!

Mop

Mop is the family's little tan dog. Sometimes they have to leave him behind with friends. But he'd much rather be running after Sammy.

Table of Contents

Chapter 1:
Surprise Lake

"Get into the boat, Mrs. Tandy. Let's go!"

As usual, Sammy was telling everyone
what to do.

His fourteen-year-old brother, Bill, said, "Hey, who put YOU in charge? Why should we take orders from a ten-year-old?"

Sammy grinned and said, "Because I'm a natural-born leader."

Bill laughed. "And all this time I thought you were just a natural-born monkey!"

Sammy splashed some water at him as he ran away.

The five members of the Woodland family were in Florida. And right now, Friday morning, they were going fishing.

Not on the ocean. The wind on the ocean was too high today.

They had rented two motorboats on Surprise Lake.

Dave Briggs, sixteen, wasn't able to walk. So he had to be lifted into a special seat by the others.

Bill Westburg, fourteen, and his sister, Kathy, thirteen, got into that boat, too.

Mrs. Tandy and Sammy sat down in the second boat.

Mrs. Tandy said, "Surprise Lake really IS a surprise.

"We couldn't even see it from the road."

Kathy said, "And here's another surprise, Mrs. Tandy.

"Listen to what the ranger told Bill and Dave and me.

"You know that swamp that runs for miles along the highway?

"We drove along it yesterday.

"Remember? It's marked Gator Gully on our map?

"Where we saw that big alligator near its nest?

"Well, one arm of this lake sticks out NEAR it."

Sammy said, "WHAT? How near?

"Could alligators get into THIS lake?

"Then what are WE doing FISHING in it?"

Kathy said, "Don't worry, Sammy. They wouldn't allow fishing if there were alligators here."

Bill said, "Anyone with brains would worry about alligators, though. Even a natural-born leader."

Dave laughed and said, "The ranger says that only one alligator was ever seen in this lake. A ten-inch baby alligator.

"And that was twenty years ago. It was fighting to stay afloat.

"Someone had it as a pet, and then they dumped the poor thing.

"It nearly drowned. Alligators need air to breathe.

"And no alligators have been seen in the lake since."

Sammy said, "I was just trying to scare YOU, Bill. I wasn't REALLY afraid. I was just fooling. Watch this."

He dipped his hand into the water to prove it. But Bill noticed that he pulled it out fast.

Dave said, "And the ranger showed us a map.

"This lake is even SHAPED a little like an alligator.

"So now they've nicknamed it Alligator Alley."

Bill said, "Well, let's go fishing."

He started the motor of his boat. Sammy started the other.

The two boats slid away from the dock side by side.

They motored to an island and turned off the engines.

Dave said, "Surprise Lake is hard to figure out.

"You can't see across it ... it's full of islands."

Mrs. Tandy said, "And the islands are covered with trees and bushes."

Bill said, "So's the lake shore."

Tangled roots and low-hanging branches reached to the water's edge.

Thick forests darkened the muddy shoreline.

Shadows fell over the water. They couldn't see to the bottom.

Bill said, "Let's fish right near this first island for a while.

"Let's see if worms look good to the fish."

They turned off their motors. They threw in their anchors and floated near each other.

They put worms on their hooks and cast out their lines.

For ten minutes, they stared into the water, hoping to see a fish.

But Kathy was still thinking about alligators.

Then, from the corner of her eye, she saw something move.

Not in the water. On shore.

She turned her head fast for a better look at it.

She was just in time to see a figure disappear into the bushes.

She said, "Hey, I saw a little girl over there!

"Why would she be alone out here?"

Dave said, "Are you sure it wasn't a deer you saw?"

Sammy heard them talking. He grinned horribly and called, "Or an ALLIGATOR, maybe?"

He snapped his teeth shut. He bent his fingers into claws. He roared.

Bill said, "You don't scare us, Sammy, but that would probably scare away any alligators."

Sammy said, "I hope so!

"Maybe another alligator got hungry ... and DID swim down Alligator Alley!

"Maybe a big one COULD do it ... if he really WANTED to.

"Alligators have to eat, too, you know!"

Mrs. Tandy said, "For goodness sake, Sammy.

"You know there isn't an alligator anywhere around here."

Dave said, "And there's not a FISH around here, either.

"Maybe we should try lures instead of worms.

"Let's see, if I were a fish, what lure would I go after?

"Probably something bright, the water's so dark."

Bill said, "I've got a little yellow lure that you can use."

He fastened it to Dave's line and called

to the other boat, "What if Dave and Kathy and I motor around the island?

"I'll call if the fish are biting on the other side."

Bill turned on the engine and they motored out of sight.

After a while, Mrs. Tandy said, "Hey, Sammy. My feet are wet!"

Sammy looked down. He said, "Hey, my shoes are soaked, too!"

He gasped, "Mrs. T! Our boat's filling with water!"

The next second he was shouting at the top of his lungs.

"Help!

"H-E-L-L-L-P!

"OUR BOAT'S SINKING!"

Chapter 2:
The Rescue

Sammy heard Bill shout back, "HANG IN THERE, SAMMY!

"BE THERE IN A SECOND!

"DON'T WORRY!"

But Bill and the others were plenty worried themselves.

They reeled in their lines fast.

They came speeding around the island to Sammy and Mrs. Tandy's boat.

Sammy grabbed hold of the side of Bill's boat.

He gasped, "We were all right a minute ago.

"Now there's water all the way up to our ankles!

"What should we do?"

Bill said, "I'm not sure, but you're OK. We can get you into our boat if we need to."

Dave said, "Listen, Sammy. I've read that some boats have holes built into the bottom ... to drain them.

"Feel around in your boat. Near the motor.

"See if there's a little hole with water

running in."

Sammy said, "What if we sink while I'm looking?"

But he leaned down. He began to feel around.

In a minute he said, "I FOUND it!"

Dave said, "Good! Plug the hole with your foot. That will slow the water.

"Then reach down again. See if there's something down there that feels like a plug.

"Maybe on a chain."

Sammy said, "You're kidding! Like an old-fashioned bathtub?"

But he stuck his arm under the water again and felt around.

Sure enough, he found a plug rolling around.

He said, "I've got it! I think it's supposed to screw in.

"But the water keeps pushing it out.

"Now what?"

Dave said, "Let me think what that book said.

"I've got it!

"Bill, you get into Sammy's boat. He might need help.

"Kathy, you take over with our boat. Keep it next to Sammy's."

Bill stepped across into Sammy's boat.

Dave said, "Now Sammy, you run your boat ... and fast.

"That will stop the water from rushing in so hard."

Sammy said, "But what if that doesn't WORK?

"What if I do it wrong?

"What about ALLIGATORS?"

Bill said, "You can do this, Sammy ... even without my help."

Sammy thought, "If Bill thinks I can do it, then I'll DO it."

14

So he started the motor. And he ran the boat so fast, it sounded like an airplane.

Mrs. Tandy shouted to him, "LOOK! The water is going down a little."

Dave shouted, "OK, Sammy! Now try to screw that plug back in!"

Sammy said, "Bill, take over the steering for a second."

Then he leaned down and screwed the plug back into the hole.

Bill said, "We're lucky Dave is such a bookworm.

"He always knows what to do in an emergency.

15

"You don't have to be scared with Dave around."

Sammy put on his bulldog face.

He said, "Scared? Scared? I wasn't scared!

"I was just pretending ... so that YOU wouldn't be the only one scared.

"Now stop gabbing!

"And let's catch some fish!"

Bill just grinned and got back into Dave and Kathy's boat.

They all dropped their lines into the water again.

Soon they had eleven fish on their stringers.

Mrs. Tandy said, "These will fry up fine."

Bill said, "Sammy, you caught the most, so you get to clean them."

Sammy said, "Well, I don't mind doing the scales.

"But I'm not doing the guts! Kathy can do that. After all, she's the one who's going to be a doctor."

Just then, they saw Kathy smile and wave toward shore.

She explained, "Look, there's that little girl I saw before.

"See, she's moving around behind those trees.

"She seems awfully shy. But I think she's staring at us!"

Mrs. Tandy said, "She's very skinny, isn't she? Do you think she's hungry?

"Maybe she would like our fish for dinner."

Sammy said, "Let's give them to her. We could have hot dogs instead."

Mrs. Tandy said, "Fine with me," and the others agreed.

They lifted up their stringers with the fish on them.

They steered their boats toward the shore.

They pulled up in front of the little girl.

She was wearing pointy cowboy boots.

Even so, she darted right into the water, out to the boats.

Water ran in over her boot tops ... but she didn't stop.

She reached out. She grabbed the two stringers.

Without saying a word, she hurried back to shore.

Then she disappeared into the dark shadows of the forest.

Chapter 3:
Poor Little Thing

Kathy said, "Wow, she must be REALLY hungry!"

Sammy said, "I'M plenty hungry right now.

"Let's turn the boats in and go get some hot dogs."

Dave said, "Good idea."

They drove over to the Happy Hot Dog Hut.

They washed up and took the hot dogs to a table.

Kathy said, "What do you suppose that little girl was doing ... all alone in the woods?"

Bill said, "She looked too young to be out there alone.

"Some older person must have been with her.

"Hey, you don't suppose people are LIVING out there?"

Sammy said, "You mean like a homeless family?"

Bill said, "I bet that's it! Did you see how ragged her clothes were?

"Poor little thing.

"Let's take some food out to her and her family in the morning.

"If we are wrong and she's not homeless, we can always use it ourselves."

Mrs. Tandy said, "That's a good idea. We didn't have anything planned until Chief Hemster's plane arrives tomorrow night."

Chief Hemster was the family's best friend.

He would be flying in to Florida on Saturday around 6:00 P.M.

Sammy said, "Poor Mrs. T. She has to live without her BOY friend for another twenty-four hours.

"And then he can only spend Sunday with her.

"He has to go to police meetings all day Monday."

Bill said, "Well, right now let's make a list of the foods we should buy for the homeless family."

Sammy said, "Here, I'll clear the table."

He picked up all their used paper napkins.

He walked behind Bill on his way to the garbage can.

All of a sudden, he stopped ... and stuffed the napkins down the back of Bill's T-shirt.

He raced around the table so Bill couldn't get him back.

Then he said, "Now, no more clowning around, Bill.

"It's time to make plans."

Bill just shook the napkins out of his shirt.

He was used to Sammy.

Dave said, "We should probably buy food in cans. If these people ARE living outdoors, they will want to keep the bugs out."

Sammy said, "Yeah. There sure ARE a lot of bugs down here!

"And I mean BUGS!

"Those palmetto bugs could scare you silly ... unless you're brave, like me."

Mrs. Tandy said, "People down here CALL them palmetto bugs.

"But they look like giant cockroaches to me!

23

"Some of them are as long as my thumb. Or longer!"

Sammy said, "Remember how Bill screamed when one crawled out of the motel closet?

"But I found one that was bigger than his.

"And I only screamed a LITTLE.

"And then I threw it out the door."

Bill said, "Yeah, but mine was alive. YOUR palmetto bug was as dead as a doorknob.

"And even so, you wouldn't touch the thing.

"You pushed it onto a sheet of paper, Mr. Brave Guy."

Dave said, "Once I saw a picture of a really huge cockroach ... a hissing cockroach.

"A kid had it for a pet. It was FOUR inches long. Or maybe even longer."

Kathy said, "I've read that regular roaches carry diseases.

"That's why you should get rid of them."

Bill said, "Well anyway ... the food we get should be in cans.

"Or single-helping plastic bags.

"Or jars."

Sammy said, "Let's get potato chips. And trail mix. And corn chips. And raisins."

Mrs. Tandy said, "How about fruit juice in little boxes? That would be easy to use."

They wrote everything down and went off to shop.

■   ■   ■

Saturday morning, the Woodlanders were ready early. They took boats out on Surprise Lake again.

Kathy said, "I wonder if that little girl is even going to turn up?"

They began to fish in the same place as the day before.

Bill said, "Keep watch on the shore out of the corner of your eye. But don't stare.

"We don't want to scare her."

In a few minutes, Dave said to Bill and Kathy, "Hey, I see her!"

He waved to signal the other boat that she was back.

On the shore stood the little girl in her pointy boots.

She was a few feet away from the water's edge.

A boy walked out of the woods and stood right beside her.

He looked older, about eleven or twelve.

The Woodlanders motored slowly toward shore.

They waved and smiled. Bill and Sammy held up the two bags of food.

The boy and girl walked down to meet them.

Bill called, "We brought you a present ... from the Woodlanders. That's us.

"We don't want to butt in ... but we thought maybe you could use a little help."

Bill and Sammy stepped out onto the shore. They tied the boats to a tree. The rest of the family stayed seated in the boats.

The boys set the bags of food down in a dry spot.

The new boy reached over and shook Bill's hand.

He said, "I'm Willie Ringer, and this is my sister, Belle."

Sammy said, "You're kidding! Her name is BELLE RINGER?"

He laughed, really loud. "HA HA HA! Belle Ringer! What a name!"

Without a word, the little girl kicked the mud hard. Mud went flying right at Sammy!

Chapter 4:
Homeless

Sammy yelled, "HEY!"

He had mud all over. Mud was dripping down his shorts. Mud was even on his shirt.

He tried to wipe it off, but he was still muddy.

In fact, he looked worse than before.

He said, "Why did she do that? What's wrong?"

Bill said, "Could be she doesn't like to be laughed at, Sammy."

Kathy leaned over the side of the boat.

She said, "You shouldn't make fun of people, Sammy."

Belle sat down in front of one of the grocery bags.

She stretched her neck and looked into it. Her eyes lit up.

She grabbed a small bag of potato chips.

She ripped the bag open and began munching.

Dave said to Willie, "We saw your sister here yesterday.

"We were worried. She looked so

little and helpless."

Sammy said, "Yeah, she's about as helpless as a mule."

He scraped some mud off his knee.

He added, "And she's got the aim of a star soccer player!"

Belle stared at Sammy like an angry cat.

Kathy said to Willie, "We thought that Belle was out here alone."

Willie said, "She wasn't alone. I was with her. Right behind her, in the forest.

"Our family lives out here now ... but not our dad.

"He got sick.

"He couldn't work, so he lost his insurance.

"And without his insurance, we couldn't pay for a hospital.

"Mom was working, so she couldn't take care of Dad at home.

"So he's gone to live with his folks till he's better."

Dave said, "But how did you end up out here?"

Willie said, "Well, after Dad left, Mom's company closed down. She didn't have a job any more.

"So we couldn't even pay our rent.

"But one of the rangers here was Dad's best friend.

"He said he needed someone to help keep the park clean.

"He gave us the job, and a place to set up camp.

"We clean up litter every day around closing time."

Kathy said, "But how do you take care of yourselves? Where do you sleep?

"Last night it poured rain for three hours."

Sammy said, "And besides, the bugs

are terrible around here."

Willie said, "Mom thought of all that. She sold our furniture. Then she bought a used tent from an army supply store.

"It's big, and it's just about watertight.

"And it's got netting over the windows and the doorway. So it's nearly bug-tight, too."

Bill said, "How long have you been living here?"

33

Willie said, "Ten weeks. We are going to stay till our dad comes back.

"Our camp is up at the end of the lake ... up toward Gator Gully.

"And Mom found a regular job at a shop here, a good one. Right near the edge of the park. And she gets to use a van from work.

"Weekdays, Belle stays at the shop with her. I walk out of the park to my old school. We get to help her on weekends."

Sammy said, "Then how come you're here today?

"It's Saturday. How come you're not at the shop?"

Willie said, "Mom had a lot of pet food deliveries to make. She found someone who can run the shop for a few hours.

"So I stayed with Belle."

Bill said, "You sure have been through hard times."

Sammy said under his breath, "Yeah, especially taking care of your little sister."

Willie said, "Mom says everything's OK now.

"She works every single day. But she says that's fine.

"She loves her job, and we need the money."

Kathy said, "What kind of business is open every day?"

Willie said, "It's a pet shop ... the biggest pet shop in this part of Florida.

"It's not really OPEN Sundays. But just the same, the pets need to be fed and watered. And the cages need to be cleaned.

"The man who used to work for the owner moved away.

"Then two boys who worked after school went out for track. So they quit.

35

"So the owner was running things by himself. And he's eighty.

"Now that Mom's at the shop, he stays home on Sundays. And sometimes Saturdays.

"Sunday is when supplies and new animals are delivered. My mom keeps track of all that."

For the first time, Belle stopped eating and looked up.

She said, "We get to play with the animals."

Then she went back to her chips.

Sammy said, "What kind of animals does the shop have?"

Willie said, "You know ... dogs, cats, rabbits, birds, guinea pigs, snakes, fish.

"Even a hedgehog."

Suddenly Belle spoke up again.

She added, "Lizards. Turtles. Frogs. Rats."

Then she clammed up. She didn't say another word.

Willie said, "Belle doesn't like to talk to strangers.

"She started kindergarten this year.

"But she didn't want to be away from us.

"Dad was gone. Our apartment was gone. Our furniture was gone.

"She was scared she'd find US gone one day when she got home.

"She was so scared, she even stopped talking for a while.

"Mom decided Belle could start school next year instead.

"But let me tell you, Belle's plenty smart.

"In fact, she's discovered some funny business at the pet shop."

Sammy said, "What did she discover?"

Willie said, "Well, it's hard to explain. It's kind of a mystery ... ."

Chapter 5:
What Belle Dug Up

"A mystery!" Sammy said. "We HAVE to hear this."

Willie said, "Maybe Belle will tell you herself.

"Tell them, Belle."

Belle stood up and cocked her head to one side, but she didn't speak. She looked like a smart little bird, listening for danger.

Then she pointed a skinny little finger at Sammy.

She said, "No. This little kid will laugh at me again."

Sammy said, "I won't laugh again, honest.

"I'm really sorry I made you feel bad.

"Sometimes kids do that to me. They tease me because I'm so big.

"See, I'm nearly as big as Bill here, and he's fourteen."

He moved over. He stood beside Bill.

Sure enough, they were almost the same height and shape.

Sammy added, "One kid calls me Big Bear all the time. And Jolly Giant. And

Extra-Large.

"You're the only one who ever called me a LITTLE kid." He smiled at her.

Belle thought that over. But she said, "Willie, you tell."

Willie said, "Well, last week I read a newspaper article to Belle.

"It said that some workers were digging in a limestone pit.

"You know, they dig up blocks of limestone to make buildings.

"Well, those guys dug up this giant armadillo skull!

"The article said that giant armadillos used to live in Florida.

"The article said that the armadillo must have been HUGE.

"It would have weighed six hundred pounds!"

Sammy said, "Come on, Willie! You're making that up!

"I've seen armadillos out west. They're about the size of basketballs."

Suddenly Belle began to stamp her foot.

She said, "He is NOT making it up!" She stepped toward Sammy.

Sammy stepped away, fast.

He said, "Oops. I take back what I said.

"He's NOT making it up! I'm SURE he's not making it up!

"I just meant it was hard to believe.

"That armadillo must have been as big as an igloo. Probably looked like one, too."

Dave said, "Hey, I read that same article.

"It said the animal lived ten thousand years ago.

"And the article said that other huge animals lived here then.

"Mammoths ... giant sloths.

"And they think that people lived here and hunted them."

Belle looked Sammy right in the eye and said, "SEE? I told you so, you big-mouth little kid!"

Willie went on with his story. "Well, Belle figured if THOSE GUYS could dig up an armadillo skull, then she could, too.

"But she didn't have a limestone pit to dig in.

"Mom said Belle could dig behind the shop. There's a wide strip of gravel back there.

"So Belle carried our camp shovel outside with her.

"Mom says that a few minutes later, Belle came running inside.

"She grabbed Mom's hand and almost dragged her out.

"Belle DID find something."

Mrs. Tandy said, "Was it a fossil of some kind?"

Willie said, "Well, not a giant armadillo skull."

Kathy said, "Then WHAT?"

Willie said, "Parrots. Three dead parrots."

Belle said, "And those parrots really STINKED!"

Willie said, "Belle's right! They DID stink.

44

"So Mom shoveled them into a big plastic bag ... and tied it shut.

"She brought them home. Then on Monday, she took them back to show her boss.

"But Mr. Worth was sick. And he's still sick. He hasn't been to the shop this week.

"So the dead parrots are back at our camp again.

"Hey, do you want to see them?   And our camp?"

Dave said, "You bet.

"But I couldn't get there from here in my wheelchair, could I?"

Willie said, "No, I guess not. But wait. There's a back road that goes near it.

"You could drive in on that.

"Then we could carry you from there to our camp.

"Or we could carry out the parrots for you to look at."

Belle held her nose when he mentioned the parrots. But that didn't stop her from eating.

She looked through the groceries again and opened a bag of corn chips.

Bill said, "Why don't we drive those heavy groceries to your camp?"

Belle said, "ROTTEN idea! That big little kid might eat them."

She lifted one of the heavy bags. Then, hugging it to her, she lugged it into the forest.

So Willie told them where to drive on the back road.

Then he disappeared into the forest with the other bag.

The Woodlanders got back into their boats.

They turned them in at the park office.

Twenty minutes later, Dave drove his hand-controlled van onto the back road. They drove for a little while until they saw the path.

Dave parked. Then the Woodlanders waited for Willie and Belle ... and the stinky dead parrots!

Chapter 6:
The Camp

After a minute, they saw the bushes move
at the side of the road.

Willie and Belle stepped out onto the
road and waved.

Bill, Sammy, and Mrs. Tandy jumped out of the van.

Dave said, "I'll wait in the van this time. You guys go on."

Kathy said, "I'm going to stay here with Dave.

"You can tell us about the camp when you come back."

Bill said, "I wish you would both come. Sammy and I could make a seat with our hands for you, Dave."

Sammy said, "Yeah, we could carry you in."

Dave said, "We'd waste a lot of time getting through those bushes. Besides, someone should stay with the van.

"But Kathy, why don't you go with them?"

Sammy laughed and said, "I'll tell you why ... because she's stuck on you, that's why."

Kathy turned stop-light red.

Bill and Mrs. Tandy both poked Sammy in the ribs.

Sammy smiled like a perfect angel and said, "Why is everyone always poking me?"

Then Sammy, Bill, and Mrs. Tandy trotted after Willie and Belle into the forest.

It was hard going.

At first, the forest seemed dark as night. They had to hold their hands up to feel their way through the darkness.

Then their eyes got used to the shadows.

They ducked under scratchy leaves and branches.

They squeezed between bushes and stepped over roots and rocks.

Finally, they saw an even darker spot behind some trees.

Up close, they could see it was a huge brown tent.

Willie and Belle stooped down. They disappeared under a tent flap.

The three Woodlanders followed them inside the tent.

Willie shined a flashlight around a big canvas room.

Three army cots stood in the center of it.

Sleeping bags rested on top of the cots.

A big, clear plastic bag lay under each cot.

There were neat piles of clothes inside the bags.

Shoes and slippers were in bags lined up along one wall.

Wooden boxes were lined up along the other walls.

Bill said, "You sure keep all this neat."

Willie said, "We have to ... if we want to find anything.

"The lake is right nearby. It's pretty warm, too. We take a bath in it every morning."

Sammy said, "You haven't seen any ... awful creatures ... any alligators up here, have you?"

Bill giggled.

Sammy said, "I know there aren't any alligators here, Billy Know-It-All. But they call this place Alligator Alley, so I'm just checking."

Willie laughed and said, "The only awful creatures we've seen around here are ants.

"That news article said that now-a-days, armadillos eat ants.

"But it said that those GIANT armadillos might have eaten more than ants.

"It said there wouldn't have been enough ants to feed them!

"It said that the ants would have had to be as big as potatoes!

"But I say, there are so many REGULAR-sized ants around here ... they could feed an ARMY of giant armadillos."

Bill laughed.

Sammy said, "Or maybe armadillos eat the OTHER kind of aunts ... the kind that marry uncles."

He laughed at his joke. Bill just made a face.

But Belle surprised them all with a giggle.

Mrs. Tandy said, "I read that if you put every animal living today onto a scale ... ten percent of the weight would be from ants."

Bill said, "Wow! Ten percent! That's ten pounds out of every hundred pounds!

"That can't be!"

Willie said, "Well, I believe it. Just step outside a minute. I'll show you ANTS!"

He pointed under a bush.

He said, "Look in that bag. That's what Belle found."

Three huge, brightly colored dead parrots lay in a clear plastic bag.

A few small, white bones lay in the bag with them.

And something alive was in the bag, too.

Willie picked up the bag to show them. It was crawling with ANTS.

Sammy said, "Yuck! That's the crawliest thing I ever saw!

"It's disGUSTing!"

Mrs. Tandy said, "What a pity those birds died. They're so beautiful."

Bill said, "Willie, could those parrots have died in the pet shop?"

Willie said, "I asked my mom that exact question.

"She said that no animal has died in the shop since she's been working there.

"And she said that the shop has never had parrots like these."

Sammy said, "Then how did the birds get buried there?

"And are there more?"

Willie said, "Well, look at the little bones in the bag. Those could be from other birds that died earlier."

Bill said, "Let's go show these to Dave and Kathy."

Willie said, "OK. But first, follow me."

He led them to the lake.

He opened the bag. He held it underwater.

They smelled a terrible smell.

The ants floated up to the top and began to tread water.

He poured out the water, and the ants went with it. Then he tied the bag closed.

The children hurried back to Kathy and Dave in the van.

They showed them the three dead birds.

Dave thought to himself, "You know ... those parrots remind me of something else I read in the paper. Not so long ago, either.

"Now, what was it?"

He couldn't quite remember ... because right then Sammy jumped onto a nearby log.

Sammy announced, "I think these dead parrots are a great mystery for the Woodlanders to solve!

"And I am the great leader, so I'll make a plan ...

"Bill! What should the plan be?"

Chapter 7:
This Is a Graveyard

Bill laughed. He said, "So THAT'S how you great leaders do it!

"You get someone ELSE to think of a plan.

"Well, let me see.

"First, I think there must be something crooked going on.

"Whoever buried these parrots did it in secret ... so that no one would know about it.

"So my next thought is, could Mr. Worth be tied up in something crooked?"

Suddenly, Belle jumped in front of Bill.

Again she stared at him like an angry cat. She was holding a bunch of leaves in her hand. Her arm flew back, ready to throw.

She said, "You take that back, you rat!"

Bill took a look at her fist full of leaves and said, "All right, already. I take it back! Sorry!"

Willie said, "Belle's right. Mr. Worth is one of the nicest people we've ever met.

"Mom says she's lucky to be working for him.

"She says she NEVER met a kinder person."

Sammy said, "Well, SOMEone buried these birds.

"They didn't just DIVE-bomb into the ground."

Dave said, "We should go talk to your mom, Willie.

"When will she be back from making deliveries?"

Willie said, "What time is it right now?"

Dave said, "Two o'clock."

Willie said, "She might be back already.

"And the shovel that Belle used is still at the shop.

"We could see if there are any other bird bodies buried there."

Sammy said, "Then ... what are we waiting for?

"Everybody get into the van! And fast!"

He jumped in himself.

He sat down on the back seat.

To everyone's surprise, Belle jumped in and sat next to him.

Willie joined them.

Kathy got in next to Dave, of course.

Mrs. Tandy and Bill climbed into the second seat.

Bill held the closed bag of dead parrots with his right hand.

He held his nose with his left.

Dave said, "All set? Everyone have seat belts on?"

He started the motor.

But before the van was in gear, a voice said, "I'm HUNgry!"

Willie said, "That's Belle for you! She looks like a flea and she eats like an elephant."

Sammy said, "Just a minute. I've got something you can have, Belle."

He wiggled sideways and felt around in his pants pocket.

He came up with a bent-up, twisted, beef-jerky stick.

He handed it to Belle.

She announced, "Sammy's really not so bad."

Then she started munching.

Sammy said, "All right, detectives, let's get going."

Willie showed them how to get to the shop.

There was a sign in front: THE WORTH-MORE PET SHOP.

Willie said, "Mr. Worth says he named it that because he has MORE animals than any shop around.

"And he wanted his name, Worth, in his shop's name.

"And his animals are so healthy, they're worth more."

Dave said, "It's the biggest pet shop I've ever seen."

Bill and Sammy pulled Dave's wheelchair out of the van. Dave lowered himself into it.

Willie opened the shop door.

Mrs. Ringer heard him.

She walked toward them from a row

of cages in the back.

She called, "Hey, it's my two best helpers!"

Belle threw her arms around her mother's waist.

Her mother turned in a quick circle. Belle's little body flew around with her mother's.

The two of them looked like a ride at an amusement park.

Willie said, "Hey, Mom, we brought some friends.

"We showed them the bird bones, and they want to solve the mystery."

The Woodlanders shook hands with Mrs. Ringer.

Mrs. Tandy said, "We saw your daughter yesterday. We thought she might be in a tough spot.

"So today we brought a few groceries for you."

Mrs. Ringer said, "That was very kind of you.

"You must be the people who gave Belle the fish.

"Thank you so much.

"We grilled them for dinner. They were perfect.

"Now about those birds," she went on.

"We can't figure out how they got there ... or why."

Dave said, "Mrs. Ringer, we wondered if there might be other birds buried around here."

Bill said, "Would you mind if we dug around to see?"

Mrs. Ringer said, "I think that's a good idea. We should find out all we can.

"Mr. Worth isn't well yet. I don't want to worry him about it."

She pointed toward the back wall and said, "There's the shovel."

Bill picked it up. They trotted out the back door.

They looked around.

Dave noticed a little hollow spot in the gravel.

He said, "Is that where you found the birds, Belle?"

She nodded yes.

Bill walked a dozen feet away from the hollow spot.

He pushed in the shovel and turned some gravel over.

He didn't have to dig any farther.

A dozen small white bones and a bright parrot wing came up in the shovel.

Bill said, "Hey everybody! This is a graveyard! A graveyard full of birds!"

Chapter 8:
Roach As in Cockroach

Sammy called out, "This is weird!"

Dave said, "I think we should stop digging ... at least until we've talked to the police.

"Something's been nagging at my memory," he said.

"I read it in a newspaper about a month back.

"It was about a certain kind of parrot from South America.

"The article said that people used to pay so much for these parrots that animal dealers caught too many.

"They caught so many that the parrots were put on the endangered animals list.

"Now they're protected by law because they're nearly extinct."

Belle said, "Extinct? The birds I found stinked!

"They stinked AWFUL!

"They were talking about MY BIRDS that I dug up!"

Willie smiled and said, "Not that kind of stinked, Belle.

"'Nearly extinct' means that these birds are dying out."

Belle said, "SEE?

"That PROVES it! They WERE talking about my birds!

"My birds died out so much, they're dead!"

Willie said, "I'll try to explain it some other time, Belle."

Kathy said, "Can we figure out who might have to get rid of dead parrots?"

Bill said, "Well, here's something I've thought of.

"What if there are some people who would STILL buy these parrots ... even though it's against the law?"

Mrs. Tandy said, "And what if they would pay even more NOW ... because the parrots are so rare?"

Willie said, "So some crook might be SMUGGLING them in!"

71

Kathy said, "And what if some birds died on the trip?"

Sammy said, "Yeah! That's it!

"A crook would have to get rid of the ones that died."

Dave said, "That's an awful lot of 'what-ifs.' But you know, they all hold together.

"Let's find out what else Mrs. Ringer can tell us."

They all trooped inside. They told Mrs. Ringer what they were thinking.

Then Dave asked her, "Have you ever seen a suspicious-looking person hanging around the shop?"

Mrs. Ringer said, "Really, no one comes to the shop except customers and animal lovers.

"Oh, and the man who brings animals and pet supplies.

"He comes every other Sunday.

"No matter how early I arrive, he's waiting in his van.

"But I wouldn't call that suspicious. He's here on business."

Dave said, "What's he like?"

Mrs. Ringer said, "Well, he's about forty, I'd think.

"He dresses well. In fact, he wears very costly clothes.

"His shirts all have fancy gold crowns on their pockets."

Belle said, "Like he thinks he's a king or something."

Mrs. Ringer went on. "Let's see ... he's tall, very tall."

Belle said, "He's so tall he's as long as an alligator.

"And his teeth are big and pointy like an alligator's.

"And his name is Roacher! Roach as in cockroach!"

Mrs. Ringer said, "Belle doesn't like him much."

Belle said, "Because he's mean. He's rude to mice."

Mrs. Ringer laughed and went on. "Well, he's usually polite to me. But sometimes he is different."

Willie said, "Yeah. Sometimes he acts as if he's in charge of everything.

74

"Like, Mom tells him where to put a heavy box.

"But he puts it in some other spot and says, 'This is better ... right over here.'

"Then she has to argue it out with him.

"Sometimes she just gives in. Then later we move it ourselves."

Mrs. Ringer said, "I suppose he must be OK, though.

"He deals with pet shops all over the state."

Willie said, "But Belle's right. I don't think he likes animals.

"He never pets them, or even talks to them."

Belle said, "And he doesn't like people, either.

"You can tell that he's stuck-up. His shirts have a crown on the pocket."

She pointed to a notice on the store bulletin board.

Under a full-color photo were the words
"ROMAN ROACHER, ANIMAL EXPERT"
and a phone number.

Belle said, "He pinned it up himself.
He didn't even ask my mom if it was OK."

The Woodlanders took a close look.

Kathy said, "He really DOES look stuck-
up ... and like he's putting on a fake
smile."

Dave said, "Maybe he has nothing to do with those parrots.

"But it's strange that he's always around before Mrs. Ringer ever gets to the shop.

"He'd have a chance in the dark to bury something."

Bill said, "Maybe the chief could give us advice about this."

He explained to the Ringers, "Our best friend is a police officer, Chief Hemster ... and he's flying into town tonight.

"He has meetings to go to on Monday ... but he's going to spend tonight and tomorrow with us."

Dave said, "I wish I had that article about those parrots.

"We could compare the picture to the birds that Belle dug up.

"If I could get onto the Internet, I bet I could find it."

Mrs. Ringer said, "Why, Mr. Worth's computer is right back here in the office.

"Follow me, Dave. Let's see what you can find."

Chapter 9:
Helping in the Shop

Mrs. Tandy said, "I'll watch you work on the Internet, Dave."

Willie called, "I'll get started cleaning the cages, Mom."

Sammy, Bill, and Kathy decided to help with the animals.

Mrs. Ringer said, "Fine. Belle and Willie can show you how to handle them. They both have a way with the animals."

The first cage was about as big as a small room.

Its walls and roof were made of heavy chicken wire.

Inside it were five kittens.

Belle called to the kittens, "We can't come in right now, but I'll play with you later."

The kittens all ran up next to the chicken wire.

Belle stuck a finger through the wire and petted them.

Then she said to the Woodlanders, "Come with me, you kids."

She led them over to a row of glass aquariums.

Some had turtles in them.

Sammy read the labels: Box Turtles. Spotted Turtles.

One aquarium held a HUGE turtle.

Sammy read, "Snapping turtle."

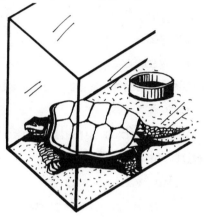

Willie said, "That guy could really hurt you!

"Snappers bite hard, and they won't let go."

Sammy said, "Some pet!"

He hurried to the next aquarium. It held small lizards.

Next to it sat a big case with a big brown lizard in it.

Sammy said, "That thing is bigger than a CAT!"

Bill said, "Look, his body is covered with scaly skin."

Sammy said, "He looks like he put on a coat of armor."

Belle led them past aquariums filled with snakes.

She picked up a small snake and petted it with one finger.

Then she whispered to the kids, "I don't want to hurt his feelings ... but reptiles aren't much fun to pet. Too dry and cold.

"Let's stick with the mammals."

Sammy said, "Hey, you're only five! And you know what mammals are! And reptiles."

Belle said, "I'm little, but my brain's

pretty big."

She took them to a big metal tub full of guinea pigs.

Brown. Black. White. Spotted. Long haired. Short haired.

Sammy said, "I love guinea pigs. But some of them bite."

Belle said, "Not these. They were hand-raised, right here.

"You can pet them, but do it from the head to the back.

"Furry animals HATE being petted from back to front."

Bill said, "Look, Willie is starting on the puppies' cages. Let's go and help."

They rushed over to Willie.

Sammy said, "I sure miss MY dog. I wish we could have brought Mop on our vacation."

Bill said, "YOUR dog? Mop is the whole FAMILY'S dog."

Sammy stuck out his tongue and said, "Yeah, but he likes me best."

In a minute, the three Woodlanders were holding puppies.

Sammy said, "NOW I know what I'm going to be when I grow up!

"I'm going to own a pet shop, with a million puppies."

The children laid fresh newspaper on the cage floors.

They cleaned out the food bowls and water pans.

They put down fresh water and more food for the puppies.

Then some small parrots nearby began screaming.

Most of them were out of their cages, on wooden stands.

One of them kept screaming, "Awk! I'm really hungry ... and don't you forget it!"

Sammy said, "Hey, it's dinner time. That's a smart parrot."

The parrot screamed, "And don't you forget it!"

Sammy said, "I won't! But you better not scream in my ear again! And don't YOU forget it!"

Bill said, "Hey, Sammy can talk parrot-talk!"

Kathy asked Willie, "How come the birds are out of their cages?"

Willie said, "They need exercise, just like us. So we keep them out most of the day."

Just then, Dave came wheeling out of the back room.

He said, "I found that parrot picture from the news article, guys.

"And it looks an awful lot like the dead parrots Belle dug up.

"I'll show you later. Right now, it's time to go meet Chief Hemster.

"Mrs. Ringer said we could bring the chief here after dinner.

"Then we can decide what to do about the buried birds."

Sammy said, "Hurry up, you guys. Mrs. Tandy doesn't want to be late to see her BOY friend!"

The parrot screamed, "And don't you forget it!"

Chapter 10:
He Could Be the One

Chief Hemster's plane came in right on time.

Passengers piled out ... but not the chief.

Bill said, "I wonder if he missed the plane?"

Sammy said, "Oh, he's on it, all right.

"He wouldn't miss a chance to see his GIRL friend."

He looked hard at Mrs. Tandy and grinned.

Mrs. Tandy grinned back and said, "Did you know the chief likes monkeys?

"So he CERTAINLY wouldn't miss a chance to see Sammy."

Just then, a noisy crowd walked through the hall behind them.

Kathy turned around.

Suddenly, she whispered, "Look! Look at that tall man! On the far side of the crowd.

"Over there. The only one who isn't carrying baggage."

The others turned their heads and looked.

Sammy whispered, "Hey. That man's the animal guy!

"It's that Roman Roacher, from the notice at the shop."

Bill said, "You're right.

"Look at that crown on his shirt pocket."

Dave said, "And see, he IS acting stuck-up, just like Willie and Belle told us.

"He's walking far apart from everyone else."

Sammy said, "And he's looking down his nose at them.

"Like he doesn't want to breathe the same air."

Just then, Mrs. Tandy said, "THERE'S the chief!

"No wonder he's the last person off the plane."

The chief didn't look like a police officer at all.

89

He was wearing a sport shirt and jeans.

He held a giant blue teddy bear under his arm.

He was holding a hanging bag in his hand.

With the other hand he was wheeling a baby in a twin stroller.

A woman was carrying the other twin in her arms.

Suddenly, that twin reached over to the chief's face.

It grabbed his nose. It twisted it sideways.

Then both twins started screaming bloody murder!

A man came running toward them. He was the twins' father.

He thanked the chief and took over with his family.

Chief Hemster stood rubbing his bright red nose.

Then he hugged the Woodlanders, hugging Mrs. Tandy last.

Sammy pointed at them and let out a loud giggle.

The chief said, "OK, Sammy. Now you blew it.

"I'LL have to eat the peanuts I saved for YOU!"

Mrs. Tandy said, "Oh, you mustn't do that, John. Peanuts are the perfect food for monkeys. Sammy really should have them."

The chief handed Sammy the peanuts and said, "Well ... OK.

"Now tell me, monkey, how's your vacation going?"

Sammy said, "Great. And do we have a lot to tell you!

"But first ... follow me to dinner. I'm the leader and I'm starved."

But Bill said, "Hold on for half a minute.

"Dave asked me to check something out first."

Bill hurried up the hall and then returned in a hurry.

He said, "I found out where that crowd came from, Dave.

"They started out on a plane that flew from Brazil to Miami.

They went through Customs in Miami, and then got on another plane to come here."

Sammy said, "Come on! We can talk geography later.

"Let's go to a restaurant right here at the airport.

"We can tell the chief everything while we eat."

At dinner, they told the chief about the Ringers ...

the pet shop

the buried parrots

... and the bones.

Dave showed him the picture and the article from the Internet.

Sammy took a big bite of his crusty roll.

He began telling the chief about Roman Roacher.

With his mouth full, Sammy said, "On the pet shop bulletin board we saw a picture of a man.

"He's an animal dealer.

"He delivers to the shop where Mrs. Ringer works.

"We think he could be the one who's burying the birds!

"And we saw him just now, here at the AIRPORT!"

A spray of crumbs shot out of Sammy's mouth. They landed on Chief Hemster's arm.

Sammy said, "Oh, I'm SORRY!" And

MORE crumbs flew out.

The chief just laughed.

He said, "Don't worry about it. I'm just grateful there wasn't any jelly on that roll.

"Now, here's what I think ...

"Somebody's burying those birds in secret.

"Dave thinks they are endangered South American birds.

"And now you've learned that Roacher was probably on a plane that came in from South America.

"Now, a person is innocent until he or she is proven guilty.

"But Roacher could very well be doing something wrong.

"Tomorrow's Sunday, and I'm on vacation until Monday.

"Maybe I can help you find out what's really going on.

"I think we'd better get on the phone to Customs right now."

Sammy said, "I know where all the phones are.

"I felt in every coin slot all the way to your plane.

"I found thirty-five cents and a paper clip."

Sammy led them right to a bank of telephones.

Chief Hemster placed a call.

They heard him explain to some one why he was calling.

Then he gave a long, low whistle and said, "What luck!

"Sure! We will meet you at the Worth-More Pet Shop in half an hour."

Chapter 11:
Let's Make a Plan

It was 8:30 P.M. when they got to the shop.

A black car and the pet shop van were parked in front of it.

There was a "CLOSED" sign on the door, but some lights were still shining in back.

Mrs. Ringer came out and led them back to the office.

She closed the office door.

Willie and Belle were there. And a strange man and woman were waiting, too.

They stood up.

The woman said, "Hello. I'm Agent Maria Jackson from U.S. Customs.

"And this is my partner, Agent Donald Bloom."

Sammy blurted out, "You're from Customs? Then how come you're wearing jeans and a T-shirt? Where's your uniform?"

Agent Jackson said, "Well, sometimes we don't like to advertise who we are."

Agent Bloom said, "You must be the

Woodland family. The Ringers told us about you.

"And you're Sammy. Belle says you're the leader, Sammy.

"She told us you can solve any problem.

"She says we should even tell you if we get hungry."

Sammy puffed out his chest. The rest of the family grinned.

Agent Jackson said, "And you, of course, are Chief Hemster.

"We were so happy when we got your call, sir.

"You see, we've been watching this man for months."

Agent Bloom said, "The Ringers filled us in on everything they know about him.

"That he's at the shop before sunrise every other Sunday.

"That he's due to make a delivery tomorrow.

"We even dug in the gravel behind the store.

"We turned up another shovelful of bones."

Chief Hemster said, "Why don't you tell us what you already know about Roacher?"

Agent Bloom said, "Well, first let me say this: he has no police record.

"We know he's a long-time dealer in tropical animals.

"He used to be well-liked, but he's changed.

"These days he keeps pretty much to himself."

Sammy said, "Why are you suspicious of him?"

Agent Jackson said, "For three main reasons.

"First, Roacher is close friends with a man in Brazil.

"That man's business used to be selling parrots ... back when it was still legal.

"Customs in Brazil suspects that this man is still selling birds ...

"And we suspect he is selling the birds to Roacher."

Sammy said, "What's the second reason?"

Agent Jackson said, "Roacher's mother is the second reason.

"She's a world-famous expert on parrots.

"She's famous for her medical work with them ... and for her work to save them from becoming extinct.

"I think you could say that she is simply WILD about parrots.

"Roacher's neighbors said his mother used to visit him often.

"But last year, she and he had a terrible fight.

"The neighbors could hear the shouting right through the walls.

"She hasn't been near his place since then.

"We think she stopped visiting him because she found out he was smuggling birds."

Sammy said, "So what's the third reason you suspect him?"

Agent Bloom laughed.

He said, "You don't let go, do you, Sammy?"

Agent Jackson said, "The third reason is that Roacher goes so OFTEN to Brazil. As regular as clockwork. Every second Thursday.

"And he always returns two days later ... every second Saturday ... as he did tonight."

Sammy said, "So why haven't you arrested him?"

Agent Jackson said, "We still haven't figured out his method of operation ... his M.O.

"We know he isn't selling protected birds to any of the pet shop owners he serves.

"So where is he selling them?

"And how is he getting them into this country?

"We've gone through every shipment

of animals and birds that he's sent. But we've never found one that was illegal."

Kathy said, "Is it possible he isn't smuggling parrots at all?"

Agent Bloom said, "It's possible, but not at all likely.

"Yet we don't want to pick him up ... even for questioning ... until we have some evidence.

"But now thanks to you, we have the birds and the bones.

"And now we know he often has a chance to bury dead birds here.

"I think you've given us much of the evidence we need.

"We will probably take him in tomorrow morning."

Chief Hemster said, "Maybe we can help. Let's make a plan right now."

Sammy said, "I wanted to come tomorrow anyway, to play with the puppies again."

Dave said, "Hey, we could ALL be here!"

Kathy said, "But what if someone drives by and sees us?"

Bill said, "So what? We wouldn't look suspicious.

"We'd look like a family out buying a pet.

"Like we couldn't come in during the week."

"We can ALL be here when Roacher comes in."

Agent Jackson said, "That sounds like a good plan.

"Roacher isn't dangerous. We know he doesn't carry a gun.

"I'll have some of our agents do a stake-out during the night.

"They'll see if Roacher buries anything out back.

"They can take pictures of what he does."

Agent Bloom said, "Then we can all show up here early Sunday morning ... like a family out to choose a puppy.

"What time do you usually open up the shop, Mrs. Ringer?"

Chapter 12:
A Quiet Sunday Morning

The next morning, Mrs. Ringer pulled up in front of the pet shop. She got out of the van and un-locked the door.

As usual, the sign on the pet shop door said CLOSED ON SUNDAYS.

Belle and Willie got out of the van and went inside with her.

Roman Roacher's big van was already parked in front.

Roacher walked right in after the Ringers.

He followed Mrs. Ringer toward the office at the back.

Then he heard another car drive up.

He swung around to look out the front window.

A third van, a big one, had just stopped in front of the store.

Two men and two women and four young people were getting out.

They were dressed in jeans and summer shirts.

They helped one boy out of the van and into a wheelchair.

They looked harmless enough.

They came inside.

Sammy was saying, "I liked that little white poodle the best.

"And it liked me.

"Did you see its stomach? It was round as a balloon!

"And it felt like a balloon, too ... a balloon full of jelly.

"We could name it Jelly Belly. Jelly, for short."

Mrs. Ringer called from the office, "Hello there, folks.

"Have you decided yet?"

Agent Bloom said, "We have to look them over again.

"We've pretty much decided that we want a dog ... not a cat.

"But we want to take another look at the puppies.

"And the kittens too.

"It's so nice of you to let us come in on a Sunday morning."

Bill said, "I want to see that black and tan sausage dog again. She's the cutest thing!

"She's almost full grown ... but did you guys see how little she is?

"And did you see how skinny her tail is?"

Sammy said, "Yeah, skinny, all right. Like a RAT tail.

"She's cute, but who wants a half-dog, half-rat?

"Jelly Belly is ALL dog."

Dave said, "But a white, fluffy dog is hard to take care of.

"You'd have to wash him all the time. And brush him."

Roacher turned back to Mrs. Ringer and said, "I'll go out and get the supplies you ordered."

He walked back through the shop's front door.

Agent Jackson, Agent Bloom, and Chief Hemster followed him out to the parked cars.

Agent Jackson announced, "I'm Special Agent Maria Jackson of the United States Customs Service.

"Roman Roacher, you're under arrest."

A look of panic flashed across Roacher's face.

Chief Hemster and Agent Bloom stood between him and his van. So he turned and ran back into the store.

As he went, he ran past a glass-sided case.

It was full of white mice.

Quick as a cat, he reached out. He pushed the case over.

Metal and glass crashed to the floor.

The mice rushed in terror in every

direction ...

over people's feet

under cases

... even into the kitten cage.

Roacher leaped over the glass. He ran toward the back of the shop.

He pushed over everything as he ran.

One after another, shelves and cases smashed to the floor.

Hundreds of animals dashed around the shop.

Lizards of all sizes darted about ... looking for hiding places.

Snakes wiggled across the floor ... trying to pick up a meal of frantic mice.

White rats chased one another into dark corners.

Hamsters darted back and forth, searching for safety.

Roacher twisted the door off a big bird cage as he ran by.

Frantic birds flew through the store.

Roacher reached the shop's back door and ran outside.

The Customs agents and Chief Hemster ran after him. But it was slow going.

They had to jump over ...

    scared animals

    spilled pet supplies

    twisted metal cages

    ... and shattered glass.

Finally, they reached the back door and ran outside.

A minute later, they rushed back in.

The Woodlanders and the Ringers were rounding up the animals.

Chief Hemster said, "I can't believe it, but we lost him.

"By the time we got out to the gravel lot behind the store, he was gone.

"Not a sign of him.

Agent Bloom said, "I've already phoned for back-up.

"If only we knew this area a little better ... maybe we could figure out which way he headed."

Belle said, "That's easy. He headed to the right."

Sammy said, "How do you know?"

Belle said, "There's the back of a long building right behind us. No doors or windows, just a solid brick wall.

"So he could only run to one of the sides."

Willie said, "And he wouldn't run to the left. There's a diner there ... and a lot of people ... even on Sunday morning."

Belle said, "So he ran to the right, into Holiday Park."

Willie said, "Belle's got it. Holiday Park is next to the pet shop.

"I have to stay here to help catch the animals.

"But Belle knows every inch of the park.

"She should go with the others, Mom. She can show them the way in the pet shop van."

Mrs. Ringer said, "Good idea. But keep close to Sammy, Belle."

Dave said, "I'll stay here. When the other agents get here, I'll bring them to the park."

Then everyone else rushed out to the van.

Chapter 13:
See You Later, Alligator

They jumped into the van and drove to
the park office.

Bill pointed to the lake and said, "Hey,
look at that motorboat out there."

Sammy yelled, "It's Roacher! He's getting away!"

Agent Jackson shouted to the ranger on duty.

The ranger ran and un-locked three boats.

The agents and Chief Hemster each jumped into one of the boats.

The chief said, "You youngsters know how to run these.

"Take over, kids."

Sammy and Belle piled in with Chief Hemster.

Bill jumped into the boat with Agent Jackson.

Mrs. Tandy and Kathy climbed in with Agent Bloom. The three boats sped off after Roacher.

Bill's boat was running a little ahead of the others.

After a minute, Bill shouted, "We

aren't gaining on him!"

Sammy yelled, "What if he steers over to the shore?

"He could run away from us into the forest!"

Belle yelled back, "So what? We'd catch him anyway!

"We'd hear him crashing and tripping and saying bad words."

In a minute, Kathy yelled, "I can't see Roacher anymore!"

Chief Hemster shouted, "I can't, either! Where did he go?"

Bill yelled back, "I saw him! He made a left turn in back of that island ... the long one that goes almost across the whole lake!"

They all turned left behind the island, too.

They expected to see him on the other side.

No Roacher.

Not even his boat!

They turned off their motors and looked around.

Belle cried out, "Hey! Where did he go?"

Sammy said, "There's nothing but a ball floating on the water.

"See ... over there? Near the lakeshore.

"Almost the size of a bowling ball."

Bill said, "That isn't a ball. The shape isn't right."

Kathy cried out, "Wait a minute!

"It's a head! A human head. It's Roacher!

"He's in the lake!

"He must have kicked out the boat plug."

Sammy said, "Just like I did Friday.

"But HIS boat went all the way to the bottom!

"I bet he's standing on the seat he was sitting on."

Roacher heard their voices.

He took one look and began swimming fast.

He was heading away from them, toward the lakeshore.

Kathy said, "He IS going to try for the forest!"

Just then, Sammy yelled at the top of his voice, "HEY, WE'D BETTER GET HIM OUT, AND FAST!

"ALLIGATOR ALLEY'S NO PLACE TO

121

BE SWIMMING!"

Bill caught on to what Sammy was doing.

He called out loudly, "AND THERE COULD BE SNAPPING TURTLES IN HERE, TOO!"

Roacher spun around.

A look of fear shot across his face.

He shouted, "ALLIGATORS? SNAPPING TURTLES? GET ME OUT OF HERE!"

He began swimming wildly toward the boats.

Bill held out an oar.

Roacher was almost close enough to grab it.

But Sammy yelled again, "First, tell us how you smuggled the birds, Roacher!"

Roacher screamed, "In my suitcase! In my suitcase!

"Now get me OUT!"

Bill and Agent Jackson hauled him up. Agent Bloom pulled his boat alongside theirs.

He had handcuffs ready.

Sammy was grinning from ear to ear. He said, "After twenty years, another alligator's been fished out of Alligator Alley!

"And this time it was a BIG one."

They motored Roacher to shore.

Dave was there waiting with more Customs agents.

They loaded Roacher into a waiting car

123

and drove him away.

Then Sammy bragged, "Ha, Dave! I got Roacher to confess how he smuggled the birds."

But Agent Jackson said, "We can't use that confession in court, Sammy.

"He was scared into confessing.

"He'd have confessed to anything, just to get out of the lake.

"But my back-up agents picked up a search warrant.

"With a warrant we have the right to search Roacher's van.

"Let's go!"

They drove back to the messed-up pet shop.

Belle went inside to tell her mother and Willie what happened.

She stayed to help finish cleaning up.

Outside, the agents entered Roacher's van.

This is what they found:

Caged animals,

Boxes of pet supplies,

And three large, brightly colored parrots in a cage. Parrots from Brazil.

Agent Bloom said, "These look just like the ones in Dave's photo."

A HUGE suitcase lay open on the van floor.

Some clothes lay in it. Some lay next to it.

Four towels lay in a pile on the floor.

Agent Bloom said, "I bet those were wrapped around the parrots.

"But there are only three live parrots here.

"He must have buried a dead one last night."

Agent Jackson said, "Customs never searched the suitcase Roacher sent through baggage.

"Who would dream he'd send live birds in it?

"It would be a death trap.

"He must have known every trip that some birds would die.

"But he didn't care."

Agent Bloom said, "I guess all he cared about was the money he'd get from selling the birds that lived."

Bill said, "I bet you'll find that poor missing parrot buried in back of the shop."

Agent Jackson said, "Roacher will go to jail for years."

Agent Bloom said, "Well, the other Customs agents will finish here. Our job is done."

Mrs. Tandy said, "Well, Chief, what do you want to do for the rest of your Sunday holiday?"

Agent Jackson said, "You'll never guess what WE are planning to do. WE are buying PETS.

"I'm getting that little sausage dog with the skinny tail. And Agent Bloom wants Jelly Belly."

Chief Hemster said, "But first, I'm buying us all lunch.

"And then the Woodlanders are taking me fishing in Alligator Alley ... now that the big, bad alligator has been pulled out."

Sammy ran into the shop to get the Ringers.

Then, laughing and talking, the Woodland family and their new friends hurried next door and had lunch.